THE NINETEENTH OF MAQUERK

Aaron Reynolds

Illustrated by Pete Whitehead

Zonderkidz

Zonderkidz.

The children's group of Zondervan

www.zonderkidz.com

The Nineteenth of Maquerk
ISBN: 0-310-70954-7

Copyright © 2005 by Willow Creek Association

Requests for information should be addressed to:
Zonderkidz, Grand Rapids, Michigan 49530

Library of Congress Cataloging-in-Publication Data

Reynolds, Aaron, 1970-
The nineteenth of maquerk : based on Proverbs 13:4 / by Aaron Reynolds ; illustrated by Peter Whitehead.
   p. cm.
 ISBN 0-310-70954-7
 1. Work ethic--Juvenile poetry. 2. Caterpillars--Juvenile poetry. 3. Conduct of life--Juvenile poetry. 4. Children's poetry, American. I. Whitehead, Peter. II. Title.
 PS3618.E965N56 2005
 811.6--dc22

                                                2004012260

Design: Merit Alderink
Art Direction: Michelle Lenger & Merit Alderink

Illustrations used in this book were created digitally using Photoshop.
The body text for this book is set in Triplex Bold and WhoaNelly.

Printed in China
05 06 07 08 09/SCC/5 4 3 2 1

People who refuse to work
want things and get nothing.
But the longings of people who work hard
ARE COMPLETELY SATISFIED.

— Proverbs 13:4

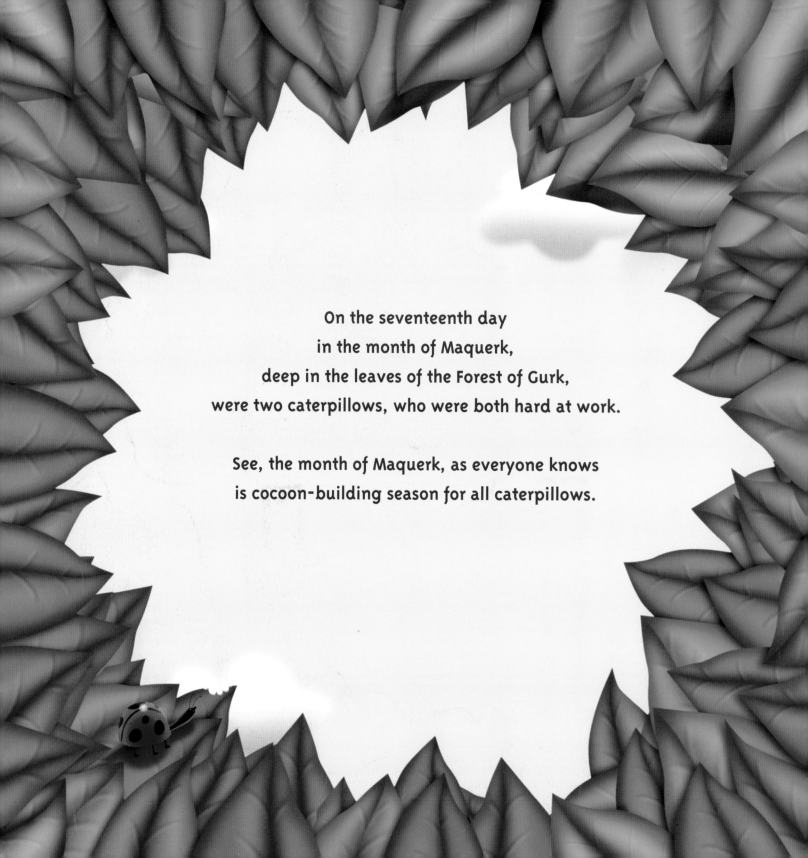

On the seventeenth day
in the month of Maquerk,
deep in the leaves of the Forest of Gurk,
were two caterpillows, who were both hard at work.

See, the month of Maquerk, as everyone knows
is cocoon-building season for all caterpillows.

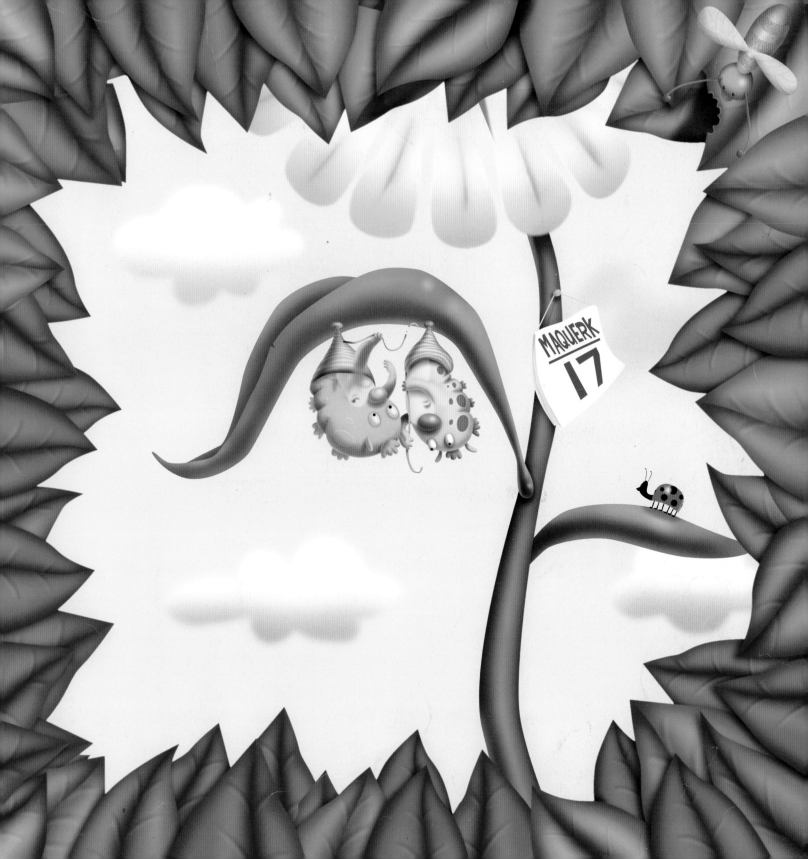

DAY 1

FOR SEVENTEEN DAYS

they had worked hard and fast
each trying to make a cocoon that would last.

DAY 9

There was still work to do.
There was much to be done.

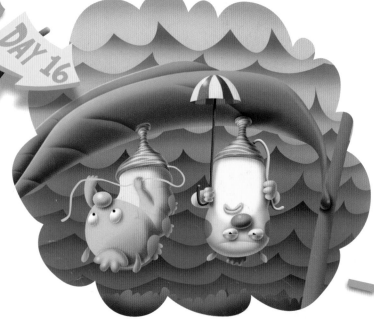

DAY 16

After all, cocoon-making
isn't always much fun.

Then the one on the right stopped his work and he said,

"I'M BORED WiTh THiS WORK. I WANT To PLAY NOW iNSTEAD!"

DAY 17

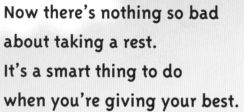

Now there's nothing so bad
about taking a rest.
It's a smart thing to do
when you're giving your best.

But a worm who thinks building
cocoons is a bore
might miss some surprises
that could be in store.

MAQUERK
17

So after seventeen days, the one on the right began to complain. AND HE STARTED TO GRIPE.

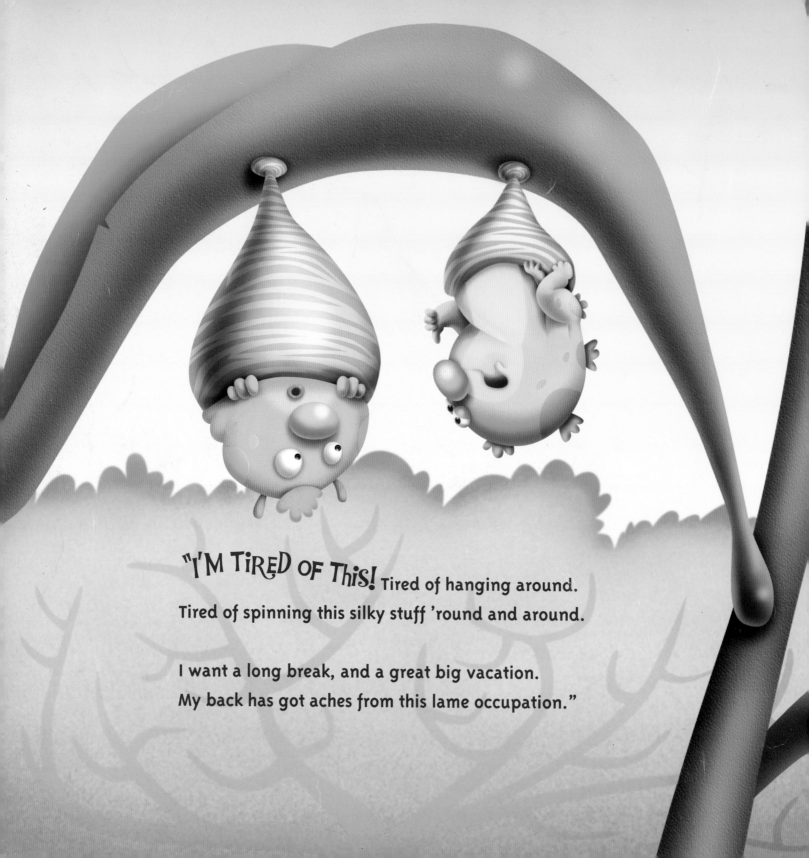

"I'M TIRED OF THIS! Tired of hanging around.
Tired of spinning this silky stuff 'round and around.

I want a long break, and a great big vacation.
My back has got aches from this lame occupation."

"A snack's what I need.
And a nap.
And a rest.
Then tomorrow I'll start back
to work quite refreshed."

So the one on the right snuggled down into bed,

WHILE WONDERFUL BUTTERFLY DREAMS

filled his head.

And as the sun set on the Forest of Gurk,
the one on the left side was still hard at work.

IN THE MIST OF THE MORN, ON THE VERY NEXT DAY,

the air was quite drizzly.
The sky was quite gray.
When the caterpillow on the right, still in bed,
looked out from his bed at the day and he said,

"What a rottenous day, so rainy and gray.
If I were a butterfly, I'd flutter away.

Well, someday I'll be one. I'll change head to feet
inside that cocoon that I need to complete."

"But a day that is rainy is spent better instead,
relaxing with covers PULLED OVER YOUR HEAD."

And this rainy gray day
in the Forest of Gurk,
the eighteenth day
in the month of Maquerk,
found one caterpillow sleeping
and one hard at work.

The next day the morning was shiny and bright
when up woke the caterpillow on the right.
But the one on the left now was nowhere in sight.

"WHERE HAS SHE GONE?"
said the right one. "Could she
be somewhere off
taking a break without me?

"If she's taking breaks on this nineteenth of Maquerk,
then I, too, deserve a nice break from my work."

So that bug on the right, feeling quite justified,
took another day off, snuggled deep down inside.

X-RAY

The one on the left, where is it she's been?
Well, I'm sure that you've guessed, she was hidden within.
Inside her cocoon—that was her location.

SHE WAS THERE GOING THROUGH BUTTERFLY-ification

And as the sun set,
on the nineteenth of Maquerk,
in the still of the eve, in the Forest of Gurk,
the one on the left had completed her work.

Now a caterpillow in the Forest of Gurk
must be in its cocoon in the month of Maquerk
on the nineteenth day—not a single day later—
or it won't change inside its cocoon change-u-lator.

MAQUERK
19

This is something our lazy friend here on the right doesn't know, BUT I BET HE'LL KNOW AFTER TONIGHT.

For the very next day, on the very next morn,
he woke up to the sound of cocoon being torn.

And lifting his covers, he saw quite a sight.
He saw his old neighbor with wings TAKING FLIGHT!
"You're the caterpillow! You're a butterfly now!
I see it, but I'm not believing it! How?"

She looked down and said,

"JUST BY SIMPLE HARD WORK,

my cocoon was complete

by the nineteenth of Maquerk."

The other one griped, "It's completely unfair,
that I'm still just me while you fly in the air!
I was cheated. Ripped off. I was brought to a halt.
My cocoon isn't done, but it isn't my fault!"

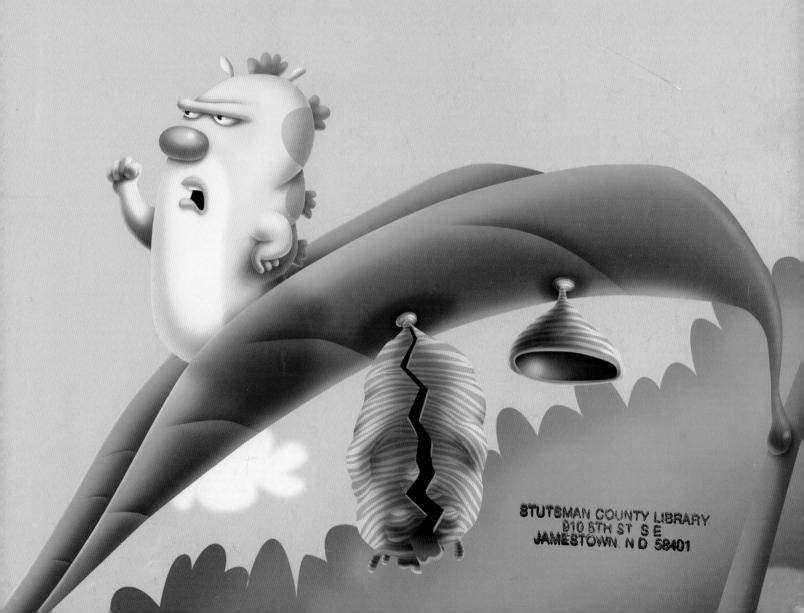

THEN THE NEW BUTTERFLY JUST fluttered away
for she had no reason to feel bad on that day.
But that sad caterpillow, the one on the right,
stayed angry and fussy long into the night.

He blamed many things—his neighbor, the rain.
He made his excuses, though he was to blame.
And he never did change, for he'd slept through the work
to build his cocoon by the nineteenth of Maquerk.

There's nothing so bad about taking a rest.
It's a smart thing to do when you're giving your best.

But a worm who thinks building cocoons is a bore
might miss some surprises that could be in store.

A bug who just sleeps instead of working should know,
he should get used to being a caterpillow.

BUSY as a BEE? OR STUCK IN YOUR COCOON?

Sometimes you'd rather just keep on resting, snug as a bug in a rug. Or playing your video game. Or watching TV. Anything, except the work that you need to do. If that's true for you, you're really missing out!

METaMORPhosiS ChaLLENGE

Next time your mom or dad asks you to do a job, try to do it happily and take it seriously. Do the very best you can. It's something called "diligence." When you work with diligence, it makes the job more fun. It feels good to do a job really well. Try it!

Sometimes good work is rewarded. Sometimes it's not. But nobody ever got a reward for whining the whole time and doing a terrible job. And who knows? In some way, just doing a good job is a little reward all by itself.

God cares about the way you work. If you don't believe it, check out Proverbs 13:4 in the Bible. Hard work pays off. If it didn't, there'd be no butterflies...and we'd all be up to our elbows in caterpillows.

MAQUERK 19

MAQUERK 4

MAQUERK 10

MAQUERK 6

MAQUERK 12

MAQUERK 1

MAQUERK 15

MAQUERK 8

MAQUERK 5

MAQUERK 13

MAQUERK 20

MAQUERK